**THIS CHRISTMAS BOOK
BELONGS TO**

....

....

HEY DUGGEE

LADYBIRD BOOKS
UK | USA | Canada | Ireland | Australia | India | New Zealand | South Africa

Ladybird Books is part of the Penguin Random House group of companies
whose addresses can be found at global.penguinrandomhouse.com.

www.penguin.co.uk   www.puffin.co.uk   www.ladybird.co.uk

 Penguin
Random House
UK

First published 2023
001

Text and illustrations copyright © Studio AKA Limited, 2023

Printed in China

The authorized representative in the EEA is Penguin Random House Ireland,
Morrison Chambers, 32 Nassau Street, Dublin D02 YH68

A CIP catalogue record for this book is available from the British Library

ISBN: 978-1-405-95379-5

All correspondence to:
Ladybird Books, Penguin Random House Children's
One Embassy Gardens, 8 Viaduct Gardens, London SW11 7BW

DUGGEE

DUGGEE'S NIGHT BEFORE CHRISTMAS

NORRIE   **ROLY**   **BETTY**   **TAG**   **HAPPY**

'Twas the night before Christmas, when all through the clubhouse, not a Squirrel was stirring, not even a mouse.

The stockings were hung by the chimney with care,
in hopes that more badges soon would be there.

TAG BETTY DUGGEE ENID

The Squirrels were nestled all snug in their beds,
while visions of Sugar Plum Duggee danced in their heads.

And Betty in her headband, and Duggee in his cap,
had just settled themselves for a long winter's nap.

When out on the lawn there arose such a clatter!
The Squirrels sprang from their beds to see what was the matter.

Away to the window they flew like a flash,
tore open the shutters and threw up the sash.

The moon on the crest of the new-fallen snow
gave the lustre of midday to hoof prints below.

When what to their wondering eyes should appear,
but a miniature sleigh and eight tiny reindeer.

With a little old driver so lively and quick,
they knew in a moment it must be Saint Nick!

More rapid than eagles, his reindeer they came.
And he whistled, and shouted, and called them by name . . .

"Now, Dasher!

Now, Dancer!

Now, Prancer

and Vixen!

On, Comet!

On, Cupid!

On, Donner

and Blitzen!

To the top of the clubhouse! To the top of the wall!
Now dash away! Dash away! Dash away, all!"

He was dressed all in fluff, from his head to his foot . . .

and his clothes were all tarnished with ashes and soot.

A bundle of badges was flung on his back,
and a Christmas one he had in his sack.

His eyes, how they twinkled! His dimples, how merry!
His cheeks were like roses, his nose unlike Hennie's!

His little red mouth was drawn up like a bow,
and the beard on his chin was as white as the snow.

He was chubby and plump, a right jolly old elf,
and they laughed when they saw him in spite of themselves.

He had a broad face and a little round belly that shook when he laughed . . .

like a bowl full of jelly.

He spoke not a word but went straight to his work
and filled all the stockings, then turned with a jerk.

And laying his finger aside of his nose,
and giving a nod, up the chimney he rose!

He sprang to his sleigh, to his team gave a whistle,
and away they all flew like the down of a thistle.

But I heard him exclaim before he drove out of sight . . .